For my unicorn-fan friends, with thanks
— S.S.

For my mom, for always believing in me
— L.M.

tiger tales
5 River Road, Suite 128, Wilton, CT 06897
Published in the United States 2019
Originally published in Great Britain 2019
by Little Tiger Press Ltd.
Text copyright © 2019 Suzy Senior
Illustrations copyright © 2019 Leire Martín
ISBN-13: 978-1-68010-176-8
ISBN-10: 1-68010-176-5
Printed in China
LTP/1800/2657/0219
All rights reserved
10 9 8 7 6 5 4 3 2 1

For more insight and activities, visit us at www.tigertalesbooks.com

UNICORN CLUB

BY SUZY SENIOR

ILLUSTRATED BY LEIRE MARTÍN

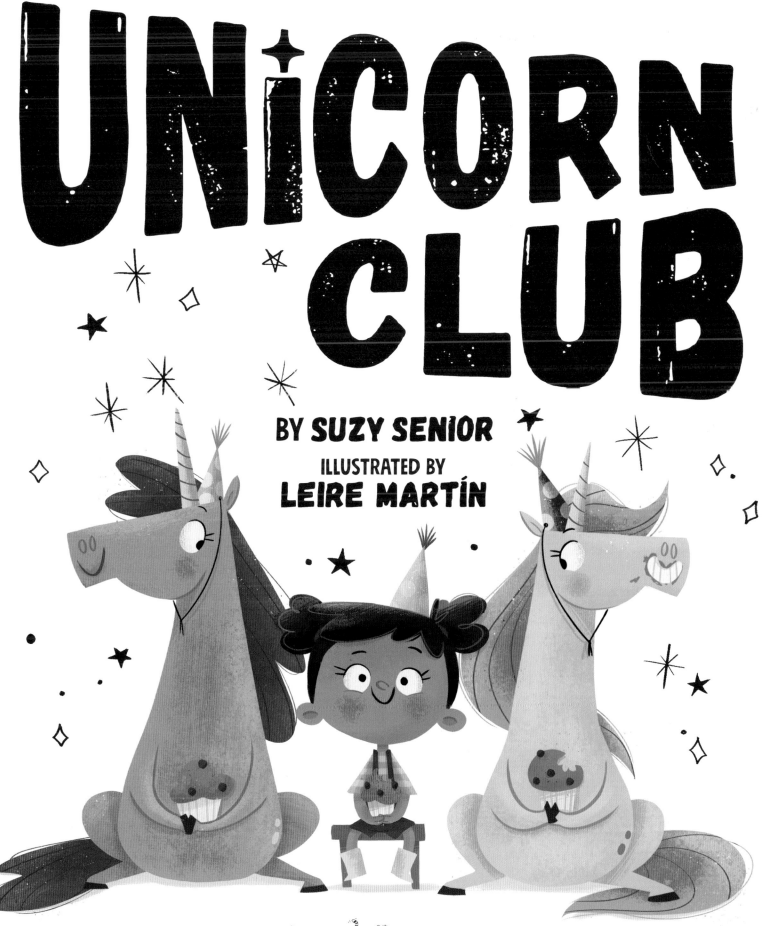

tiger tales

Saturday morning felt full of excitement.
Saturday morning was sure to be great!
Amy was starting a unicorn fan club —
The poster was ready and taped to the gate.

UNICORN CLUB
is today in the
tree house.
Everyone welcome!
At quarter past 10.
Crafts and a snack
and just 10¢
admission.

It said, in big letters, in shiny pink pen.

Amy was waiting — she jumped and she jiggled.
She nibbled a cookie and leaned on the gate.
No one was coming! The whole street was empty.
Her friends had forgotten — or else they were late.

Her Unicorn Club was a total disaster!
She finished her cookie and tried not to cry.
She pulled down the sign and went round
to the tree house . . .

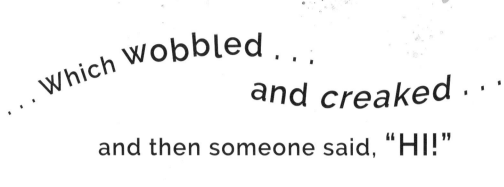

. . . Which wobbled . . .

and creaked . . .

and then someone said, "HI!"

A pink hairy face filled the tree house's window.
A big silver bottom poked out of the door.
A tail swished impatiently over the railing.
A clatter of hooves seemed to rattle the floor.

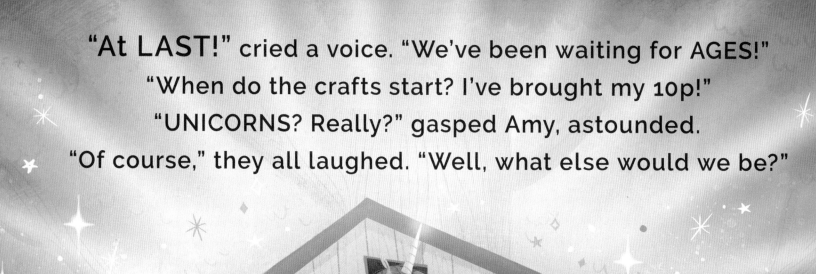

"At LAST!" cried a voice. "We've been waiting for AGES!"
"When do the crafts start? I've brought my 10p!"
"UNICORNS? Really?" gasped Amy, astounded.
"Of course," they all laughed. "Well, what else would we be?"

The smallest squeezed out and he slid down the ladder.
His glorious horn sparkled bright in the sun.
"I'm Legend," he whinnied and nuzzled her elbow.
"I reckon your Unicorn Club will be fun!"

So Amy thought fast: "You're too big for the tree house."
She ran to the garage and beckoned them in.

She got out the crayons and glitter and paint pots.
The unicorn crafts were about to begin!

They stomped and they sparkled on huge bits of paper.
They painted and pottered, and glittered and glued.

Then Legend got hungry: "What snacks are we having?"
And Amy rushed off to find unicorn food!

The unicorns crunched
and they snuffled and slobbered –
For magical beasts, they
weren't very polite –

Until they were done
and the food was demolished,
And then they licked Amy
with total delight.

"Okay," giggled Amy, "it's time for some dancing,
with ribbons to win for the funkiest moves."
They wriggled and rocked, and they rolled on the floorboards.
They disco-ed and boogied and kicked up their hooves.

"Fantastic!" said Amy. "I can't choose a winner.
Let's ALL have a ribbon." She passed them around.
The unicorns neighed and tossed their manes proudly.

But . . . "Oh!" — Amy saw something squashed on the ground.

"What's wrong?" Legend asked, trotting over to help her.
"My chalk!" Amy sniffed, staring into the tub.
"I wanted to brighten our room with a mural."
"Hang on . . . ," Legend grinned. "This is UNICORN Club!"

He lowered his head and his horn started glowing. The air seemed to shimmer with colors and light.

Then WHOOSH!

they had brushes and jars full of rainbows!
They all got to work . . .

. . . and it soon looked **JUST RIGHT!**

So, Saturday morning was full of excitement!
Saturday morning turned out to be great.
The Unicorn Club is completely amazing.
They're meeting next weekend —
and Amy can't wait!